THE WAR OF THE WORLDS

by
H. G. Wells

Teacher Guide

Written by
Pat Watson

Note

The Bantam Books paperback edition of the book, ©1988, was used to prepare this guide. The page references may differ in other editions.

Please note: Please assess the appropriateness of this book for the age level and maturity of your students prior to reading and discussing it with your class.

ISBN 1-58130-702-0

Copyright infringement is a violation of Federal Law.

© 2000, 2004 by Novel Units, Inc., Bulverde, Texas. All rights r... translated, stored in a retrieval system, or transmitted in ... photocopying, recording, or otherwise) without prior written ...

Photocopying of student worksheets by a classroom teacher a... for his/her own class is permissible. Reproduction of any part... system, by for-profit institutions and tutoring centers, or for c...

Novel Units is a registered trademark of Novel Units, Inc.

Printed in the United States of America.

To order, contact your local school supply store, or—

Table of Contents

Summary 3

Characters 3

About the Author 4

Initiating Activities 5

Book One, Seventeen Chapters 6
  Each section contains: Summary, Vocabulary,
  Discussion Questions, and Supplementary Activities

Book Two, Ten Chapters 13
  Each section contains: Summary, Vocabulary,
  Discussion Questions, and Supplementary Activities

Post-reading Discussion Questions 18

Post-reading Extension Activities 19

Assessment 25

Glossary 26

Skills and Strategies

Writing
Compare/contrast, poetry, journal entries, reflection, summary

Literary Elements
Characterization, simile, metaphor, setting, theme, plot development, allusion, personification

Listening/Speaking
Discussion, dramatizing, music, presenting

Vocabulary
Target words, definitions, application

Comprehension
Cause/effect, predicting

Thinking
Research, compare/contrast, analysis, critical thinking, current events

Across the Curriculum
Art—caricatures, sketch

Genre: Science Fiction

Setting: England; late 1890s

Point of View: first-person

Themes: fear, survival

Conflict: man vs. extraterrestrial beings

Style: narrative

Tone: pessimism (human nature, the future)

Date of first publication: 1898

Summary

An unnamed narrator recounts the tale of the invasion of England by Martians. When the unsuspecting and disbelieving humans realize their country has been invaded, they struggle to survive amidst the chaos and confusion. Using devastating weaponry, the Martians stride unchecked through the country but are ultimately defeated by their lack of resistance to human diseases. The book is divided into two sections. Book One, "The Coming of the Martians," tells of the Martians' triumphant invasion. Book Two, "The Earth Under the Martians," tells of the struggle to survive after Martians overtake the country and the ultimate demise of the Martians. Note Wells' "prophetic" correlation of the Martians with industrial robots and the descriptions of gas warfare and laser-like weapons.

Characters

narrator: unnamed, ordinary citizen; intellectual, writer of philosophical material; married; survives

narrator's wife: survives

Ogilvy: well-known astronomer; observes launching of first missile from Mars but believes he is seeing a shower of meteorites or a volcanic explosion; does not believe anything manlike can live on Mars; initially attempts to communicate with Martians and dies

Henderson: London journalist; sends telegram about invasion to his newspaper; dies with Ogilvy

Stent: Astronomer Royal; dies with Ogilvy

the curate: self-centered assistant clergyman who becomes the narrator's companion in the struggle to survive; believes Martians are God's ministers of punishment

narrator's younger brother: narrator reveals part of tale through brother's experiences; brother escapes to Belgium

Mrs. Elphinstone and her sister-in-law, Miss Elphinstone: refugees from London; narrator's brother assists them in escape

the Martians: creatures who exist inside monstrous metal machines; use Heat-Ray weapons and poison gas

About the Author

Personal Information: H. G. Wells was born in 1866, in Bromley, Kent. He spent the years 1880-1883 apprenticed to a draper in Windsor and Southsea. In 1883, he received a scholarship to further his education at the Normal School of Science in London. He studied under biologist T. H. Huxley, and his interest in biology later influenced his writing of science fiction. Following a short teaching career, he became a full-time writer in 1893. He married his cousin Isabel in 1891, but left her to marry one of his students, Amy Catherine, in 1895. He married a young English author, Rebecca West, in 1914. He died in 1946.

Literary Career: Wells became well known with the publication of his first major fiction work, *The Time Machine*, in 1895. He followed this with *The Island of Dr. Moreau* (1896), *The Invisible Man* (1897), and *The War of the Worlds* (1898), which is perhaps his most famous work. Later fiction works include *Love and Mr. Lewisham* (1900) and *The New Machiavelli* (1911). He also published several non-fiction works, including *The Outline of History* (1920), *The Science of Life* (1929-1939), and *Experiment in Autobiography* (1934). Wells continued to write prolifically, producing his last work, *Mind at the End of Its Tether*, in 1945. In addition to his literary pursuits, he joined the socialist Fabian Society in 1903; he was a member of the Research Committee for the League of Nations, publishing several books about the world organization; and he was a Labour candidate for Parliament.
Additional information can be accessed: **http://www.kirjasto.sci.fi/hgwells.htm**

Historical Background: In *The War of the Worlds*, Wells draws some parallels between the Martians' strategies with earth's inhabitants and Britain's treatment of its colonies. For example, the British almost eliminated native Tasmanians when they turned Tasmania, an island located off the coast of Australia, into a penal colony. (See Chapter 1, pp. 4-5.) Wells also drew inspiration from another specific occurrence, Mars' close position to Earth in 1894. This led to much observation and discussion, including Italian astronomer Giovanni Schiaparelli's report of seeing "channels" on Mars and M. Javelle's claim of seeing a strange light on the planet. Both "observations" stimulated speculation about life on Mars. Perhaps the most important historical event that influenced Wells to write *The War of the Worlds* was Germany's unification and mobilization of its military forces. Several English novels of the late 1800s written in semi-documentary form predicted war in Europe. Wells used this form by setting his tale of extraterrestrial warfare in specific places in England.

Correlating Material: On October 30, 1938, between 8 and 9 o'clock, Orson Welles presented a radio dramatization of Wells' novel on the "Mercury Theatre on the Air," station WABC and Columbia Broadcasting System's coast-to-coast network. Although the broadcast was preceded by a newspaper listing of the program and an introduction stating that the material was based on H. G. Wells' *The War of the Worlds*, mass hysteria gripped thousands of listeners as they interpreted the broadcast literally and believed that Martians had invaded the United States. A copy of the radio script is available at some bookstores and through mail-order catalogues.

There is also a film adaptation based on Wells' radio version of the Martian invasion (Paramount Pictures, 1953, 85 minutes; stars Gene Barry as Clayton Forrester [correlates with unnamed narrator in novel]).

Initiating Activities

Use one or more of the following to introduce the novel.

1. Have students research the effect of new technological advancements on life in the late 1800s. Discuss why Wells may have chosen to write a story about an alien invasion to voice his concerns about the effect of these changes on humankind.

2. Play a recording of the 1938 radio dramatization of *The War of the Worlds.* Would this recording affect people today the way it affected people in 1938? Why or why not?

3. Place the sentence, "Martians invade the earth" on an overhead transparency. Brainstorm with students: emotions, possible details, survival techniques, etc.

4. As a class, using the overhead transparency, write a five-senses poem about "terror."

5. Discuss stories or novels students have read or movies they have seen about extraterrestrial beings and/or their invasion of earth.

Book One
Chapters 1-3, pp. 3-15

Astronomers observe an unusual, great light on Mars but are unconcerned because they believe no life exists on the planet. A cylinder, identified as "the Thing" falls to earth. Sounds emanate from the object, and a group of men investigate.

Vocabulary

mortal (3)	nebular (3)	attenuated (4)	heath (9)
incrustation (10)	cylinder (11)	astronomical (13)	oxide (14)
extraterrestrial (14)			

Discussion Questions

1. Discuss the facts and the assumptions about Mars in the last years of the nineteenth century. *(Facts: Mars revolves around the sun at a mean distance of 140,000,000 miles, receives barely half of the light and heat from the sun as received by earth, is scarcely one-seventh the volume of earth, and apparently has water and air. Assumptions: some believe no life exists on Mars, others believe that, if any life exists, it is inferior to earth's inhabitants; Mars is nearer its end than earth. pp. 3-4)*

2. Analyze the anomalies that astronomers observe on Mars and the astronomers' speculation. *(They observe a great light and jets of fire heading towards earth, a flame each night for ten nights. The astronomers speculate that meteorites might be falling or a huge volcanic explosion occurring, but are unconcerned because of the belief that no, or inferior, life exists on Mars. pp. 5-7)*

3. Discuss the first falling "star": where it lands, what Ogilvy observes, observers' conclusions. *(It is seen early one morning rushing over and above the countryside; falls on Horsell Commons, making an enormous hole and lying almost buried in the sand; a huge cylinder with a diameter of about thirty yards; hear a stirring noise inside and see circular top rotating, indicating something is inside. Conclusions: men in the cylinder, half roasted to death and trying to escape; silence leads to conclusion that the cylinder contains dead men from Mars. pp. 9-12)*

4. Analyze the reaction of the people to the cylinder. Compare with the way people today react to unusual occurrences such as the impending eruption of a volcano. *(A crowd of people gathers, curious and impatient to see it opened; carnival-like atmosphere with food and drinks; oblivious to any danger. Today: people often do not take news seriously and refuse to leave their homes until too late. pp. 13-15)*

Supplementary Activities

1. Have students research and report on one or more of the following: European conquest of Tasmania (p. 5), invention of bicycle (p. 7, narrator learning to ride), the story of Pandora's Box (p. 14, impatience to see cylinder opened).

2. Have students apply the saying, "the calm before the storm" to the statement, "It seemed so safe and tranquil" (p. 8). Discuss the students' predictions about events to follow.

© Novel Units, Inc.   All rights reserved

3. Analyze the literary devices: **Similes**—they were scrutinized and studied...as a man with microscope might scrutinize transient creatures that swarm and multiply in a drop of water (p. 3); creatures who inhabit earth...as alien and lowly to them [Martians] as monkeys and lemurs are to us (p. 4) **Metaphor**—earth: morning star of hope (p. 4)

Chapters 4-6, pp. 16-25

Martians emerge from the cylinder, and a crowd gathers to watch. Streams of fire from the Martians' Heat-Ray decimate the humans they touch.

Vocabulary

terrestrial (17)	aperture (18)	apex (19)	intimation (20)
deputation (20)	parabolic (23)		

Discussion Questions

1. Describe the creature that emerges from the cylinder and discuss the events following its appearance. *(As the cylinder opens, observers see something grayish and billowy stirring within and two luminous disks resembling eyes, followed by something resembling a coiling gray snake and, finally, a big gray, round bulk the size of a bear. The creature has two large eyes, a rounded head with the semblance of a face, a dripping mouth, Gorgon groups of tentacles, and a covering of oily brown skin. Terror and curiosity grip the narrator and other observers, and a shopman who falls into the pit dies. A deputation of men attempts to communicate with the creatures. The Martians use a Heat-Ray that emits a stream of fire, and eventually 40 people die from the flashes of flame. The narrator escapes in terror. pp. 17-23)*

2. Discuss the methods of communicating the news and compare with today's technology. *(The news is first spread to surrounding communities by word-of-mouth. Stent and Ogilvy, who died in the first onslaught, had earlier telegraphed the news and asked for the assistance of soldiers. Today: cell phones, national on-the-spot news teams, e-mail, etc. pp. 23-25)*

Supplementary Activities

1. As a class, do a composite drawing of the creature that emerges from the cylinder.

2. Have students write an on-the-site news report about the landing of the Martians.

3. Note the literary devices: **Similes**—it glistened like wet leather (p. 17); the intense heat they project...much as the parabolic mirror of a lighthouse projects a beam of light (p. 23); they must have bolted as blindly as a flock of sheep (p. 25) **Metaphors**—I was a battleground of fear and curiosity (p. 19); beam of light: invisible hand (p. 24) **Allusion**—Gorgon (p. 17)

Chapters 7-9, pp. 26-38

The narrator escapes to his home. People in other parts of England are apathetic to the news of the Martian landing. A second cylinder falls to earth. The Martians become more aggressive. The narrator takes his wife to Leatherhead for refuge.

Vocabulary

incongruity (27)	erethism (29)	canard (30)	indefatigable (32)
cordon (32)	lassitude (33)		

Discussion Questions

1. Discuss the effect of the events on the narrator and compare the "world" at Maybury, just two miles away, with what he leaves behind at the site of the Martian landing. *(He feels as if he is in a dream. He is haggard and fearful, yet believes the Martians have done a foolish thing and is confident that they can be destroyed. His wife believes his report. At Maybury, everything seems real and familiar, and people are laughing about the reports of creatures from Mars. The world behind is frantic and fantastic. pp. 26-29)*

2. Analyze the newspaper's failure to report the message sent by Henderson. Compare with a similar situation students think might occur today. *(Henderson's report was considered to be a hoax and the editors wired him for authentication. Since he had died in the initial encounter, the paper received no reply and decided not to print a special edition. p. 30)*

3. Contrast the reactions of the citizens with those of the military authorities. *(Citizens go on about life as usual. A few seem excited, but most are unconcerned. The military takes the issue seriously and calls for reinforcement troops and weapons. pp. 31-32)*

4. Discuss Saturday's events. *(The Martians become more aggressive, setting fire to everything within range of their Heat-Ray, and reports of deaths continue. Attempts at destroying the Martians with cannons are ineffective. Military personnel go from house to house warning people to leave. The narrator takes his wife to Leatherhead for refuge but intends to return to Maybury and the site of the landing. pp. 33-38)*

Supplementary Activities

1. Analyze the metaphor, "His [the Martian's] own body would be a cope of lead to him" (p. 28). Correlate with the lead capes the hypocrites must wear in Canto 23 of Dante's *Inferno*. Elicit student response for "copes of lead" with which people might be clothed today.

2. As a class, compare the narrator's allusion to the extinct dodo bird (p. 29) with what is happening to humans.

3. Note the literary devices: **Similes**—a light-ray like the beam of a warship's searchlight (p. 31); cylinder sticking into skin of Earth like a poisoned dart (p. 31) **Allusion**—fishers of men (p. 34), Bible, Matthew 4:19 (note play on words)

Chapters 10-11, pp. 39-49

The narrator returns home and narrowly escapes death by a Martian. A third cylinder falls to earth. Fiery chaos sweeps the countryside.

Vocabulary

insensate (42)   repugnance (43)   conflagration (45)   lethargy (46)

Discussion Questions

1. Discuss why the narrator wants to return to Maybury after taking his wife to safety in Leatherhead. Elicit student response about whether or not this is typical of human nature. *(He is curious and excited about the "war" with the Martians, feels they will be annihilated, and wants to be in "at the death." pp. 39-40)*

2. Examine the imagery of the storm and correlate with the gathering war storm. *(The gathering thunderstorm clouds mingle with black and red smoke coming from the fires perpetrated by the Martians. A third falling cylinder pierces the storm clouds, and thunder sounds like exploding rockets. Hail strikes the narrator's face, and lightning flashes reveal the Thing—a walking engine of glittering metal striding across the countryside. Lightning also reveals the body of the innkeeper from whom the narrator took the cart and horse. The narrator is deluged with a storm of emotion. pp. 40-45)*

3. Describe the Martian machines and discuss the effect of the night's events on the narrator. *(Machines: monstrous bodies of machinery on a tripod stand; higher than many houses; ropes of steel dangling from them; long, glittering tentacles; brazen hood; main body followed by huge mass of white metal; huge puffs of green smoke squirting from joints; howls of "Aloo!" coming from them. Effect of events: crouches at foot of staircase in his house, shivering violently. pp. 41-44)*

4. Discuss what the narrator observes after the thunderstorm passes. Compare with pictures of the aftermath of bombing, e.g., London during WWI. *(Huge black shapes busily moving about, whole country in their direction on fire, tangy burning smell, burned houses, a wrecked train, many people hurrying away, three gigantic black things moving around. He describes the scene as a fiery chaos, and the next morning he sees a "valley of ashes." pp. 45-46)*

5. Discuss the soldier's report and his observations. *(He sobs as he tells the narrator that the Martians wiped out his unit and burned everything. He escaped because his horse fell and threw him into a depression of the ground. He observed the Martians striding over the countryside after their triumph. Most of the few citizens who survived were scalded and burned. pp. 47-49)*

Supplementary Activities

1. Have a student volunteer sketch the Thing.

2. Note the literary devices: **Similes**—driving clouds...pierced as it were by a thread of green fire (p. 40); thunder burst like a rocket (p. 40); trees parted as brittle reeds are parted by a man thrusting through them (p. 41); its [Martian's] headlike hood turning about like head of a cowled human being (p. 48) **Allusions**—Titan (p. 48); reference to "pillars of fire" (p. 49), Bible, Exodus 15:21-22. Note irony of this allusion. The pillar of fire in Exodus was used to guide and liberate the Israelites; the pillar of fire in the novel is used for extinction.

Chapters 12-13, pp. 50-64

The Martians expand their devastation. An artillery shell destroys one Martian. The narrator narrowly escapes and joins with a curate in their flight from the Martians.

Vocabulary

theodolite (51)	heliograph (51)	assiduously (52)	omnibus (53)
sabbatical (53)	obliquely (55)	curate (62)	

Discussion Questions

1. Discuss the narrator's decision, his rationale, the problems, and the final solution and outcome. *(Decision: to return to Leatherhead, get his wife, and leave the country. Rationale: country about London will become scene of disastrous struggle before Martians can be destroyed. Problem: a third cylinder, with its guarding giants, lies between him and Leatherhead. Solution: travel with soldier, eventually each going separate ways. Outcome: the two men encounter attitudes ranging from fear to disbelief, try to warn people of impending disaster, realize the fighting has begun, observe attacking Martians. Narrator plunges under water, then narrowly escapes death after the water begins to boil. pp. 50-59)*

2. Discuss the death of the Martian. *(An artillery shell strikes it in the face, tearing off the hood. The Martian blunders on, finally collapsing with great force into the river, and the impact of the Heat-Ray creates a huge tidal wave, bringing death and terrible destruction. pp. 56-57)*

3. Examine the circumstances leading to the narrator's union with the curate and the curate's summation of the destruction by the Martians. *(They meet after the narrator, injured and ill, escapes the battle scene in a boat and lands on the Middlesex bank. He dozes and awakens to see the curate, who tells him the Martians are God's ministers of wrath. They decide to go north together. pp. 61-61)*

4. Examine the curate's references to God's judgment and the narrator's response. *(Note the following statements: "...fire, earthquake, death...as if it were Sodom and Gomorrah" (p. 62), based on Genesis 18:20-28; "The smoke of her burning goeth up for ever and ever!" (p. 63), based on Revelation 18:9 and 19:3; "This must be the beginning of the end...the great and terrible day of the Lord!" (p. 63), based on Joel 2:11, 31. Narrator's response: asks what good religion is if it collapses under calamity, reminds curate of natural disasters, and tells him God is not an insurance agent. pp. 63-64)*

Supplementary Activities

1. Have a student volunteer to sketch the scene, or as a class, create a collage depicting the horrors of the Martian invasion.

2. Bring to class pictures of the large, box-like cameras of the late 1800s and early 1900s. Compare with the description of the Heat-Ray (p. 52).

3. Have students analyze the simile, "But the Martian took no more notice for the moment of the people running this way and that than a man would of the confusion of ants in a nest against which his foot has kicked" (p. 56).

4. Note the literary devices: **Metaphors**—twelve-rounder guns: bows and arrows (p. 53); beam of Heat-Ray: lightning (pp. 52-53). **Similes**—[Martians] as fast as flying birds (p. 55); the splashes...sounded like thunderclaps (p. 56); decapitated colossus reeled like a drunken goat (p. 57); yelling like siren (p. 57); people scrambling out of water like little frogs hurrying through grass (p. 58) **Personification**—Death is coming! (p. 53)

Chapters 14-15, pp. 65-81

The story switches to the second-hand experiences of the narrator's brother. News of the Martians creates confusion and chaos in London, and the brother joins other fugitives who are leaving London. The Martians employ poisonous vapor that kills all who breathe it. The fourth cylinder falls.

Vocabulary

menagerie (67)	terminus (68)	quasi (70)	nomadic (71)
tocsin (72)	ejaculating (74)	ululation (76)	

Discussion Questions

1. Discuss the change in the narrative technique. Elicit student response concerning why Wells changes the technique at this point of the story and whether or not they think the change is effective. *(Narrative switches to second-hand experiences of narrator's brother, enabling the reader to get a different perspective of the invasion. The brother's experiences tell of his and others' exodus from London and the encroaching terror of the Martians. Throughout Chapters 14, 16, and 17)*

2. Compare the atmosphere in London with the reality of the Martian invasion and discuss what changes the attitude of Londoners. *(Although newspaper accounts report the invasion and some deaths, they calm the fears and discourage panic by stating that the Martians have not left their pit nor appear to be capable of doing so, by pointing out that this small number of Martians would not be able to overpower the millions of humans, and by assuring the people they are safe. Most people are optimistic, and some joke about the invasion. Refugees from the Weybridge and Woking areas begin to relate the reality of the invasion, and ensuing newspaper accounts give first-hand information. Londoners begin to panic as they hear the reports and see the approaching fire and smoke. pp. 65-74)*

3. Examine the Martians' strategy and weaponry. *(They advance in a line, separated by about a mile and a half from each other. They communicate through siren-like howls. They use thick black tubes to discharge canisters of poisonous gas that covers the countryside with a lingering black cloud that brings death to all who breathe it. pp. 75-81)*

4. Analyze the implication of the statement, "No doubt the thought that was uppermost...was the riddle—how much they understood of us" (p. 77). *(Student response will vary. Point out that this is the question we ask in many situations, that spies ferret out such information during wartime, and that defense strategies depend on the answer to the riddle.)*

5. Note the foreshadowing of the statement, "At that time no one knew what food they needed" (p. 77). The feeding techniques of the Martians are explained in Chapters 2 and 3 of Book Two (see pp. 113 and 121-122)

Supplementary Activities
1. Bring to class articles and/or pictures about the use of poison gas in WWI. Compare with Wells' account of the Martians' use of the gas.

2. Note the literary devices: **Metaphor**—Martians: boilers on stilts (p. 70) **Similes**—sound like the distant concussion of a gun (pp. 77-78); houses rising like ghosts (p. 79)

Chapters 16-17, pp. 82-100
The Martians advance. The narrator's brother assists two ladies in the flight from London. They escape by boat to Ostend, Belgium. The narrator alludes to the fifth cylinder, and the sixth and seventh cylinders fall.

Vocabulary
coherency (82)	stalwart (83)	pugilistic (84)	paroxysm (86)
torpor (89)	volition (92)	rout (93)	ramifications (94)
chaffering (96)	exorbitant (97)	leviathan (98)	

Discussion Questions
1. Discuss the "roaring wave of fear" that sweeps through London. Note the statement on p. 89, "...certain things all that host had in common...fear and pain." Analyze the universal reactions to panic. *(People begin to flee London in massive numbers, causing congestion and panic at railway stations and shipping ports. Panic overcomes rationality as people fight savagely for every means of transportation, and many are trampled and crushed. All organization, including the police, is lost. Universality: self-preservation; panic during fire, etc., when people are trampled to death trying to escape. pp. 82-92)*

2. Discuss the assistance the narrator's brother gives two ladies and note how tragedy delineates social lines, etc. *(He defends Mrs. Elphinstone and her sister-in-law against a robber and drives their carriage through the confusion until they reach the coast, thus providing his own transportation. Other refugees along the way include the wealthy and the poor, the young and the old, all trying to escape the menace of the invading Martians. All are thirsty, hungry, and deathly afraid. pp. 83-92)*

3. Discuss the events that transpire when the narrator's brother and the two women reach the coast. *(They find a wide array of shipping vessels there, with greedy captains bargaining for more money. A warship, the* Thunder Child, *is anchored about two miles out. The narrator's brother secures passage on a steamboat going to Ostend, Belgium. Martians appear and enter the ocean shortly after the ship sets sail. The* Thunder Child *charges at the Martians full speed and fires, causing the Martians to retreat toward the shore. A Martian fires his Heat-Ray at the warship and the* Thunder Child *explodes, causing a Martian to crumple. The steamboat escapes. pp. 93-100)*

4. Analyze the object the steamboat captain and the narrator's brother see. *(Responses will vary. Ask students to consider what it might be and why it "rain[s] down darkness upon the land." p. 100)*

5. **Prediction:** Do the narrator's brother and the two women reach safety?

© Novel Units, Inc.   All rights reserved

Supplementary Activities
1. Brainstorm with students the effect of 6,000,000 people exiting London at one time. Compare with the Biblical account of the exodus of the Israelites from Egypt (book of Exodus), also portrayed in the movie *The Ten Commandments*, or with another mass exodus in history.

2. Note the literary devices: **Similes**—crowd roared like a fire (p. 87); network of streets spread like a huge map (p. 93); crumpled him up like a thing of cardboard (p. 99) **Metaphors**—human throng: swarming of black dots (p. 93); mass of human beings: current (p. 93); fleet of warships: serpent of black smoke (p. 96)

Book Two
Chapters 1-2, pp. 103-117

The narrator and the curate escape and take refuge in a house, where they are imprisoned when the fifth cylinder strikes it. They observe the Martians' activities.

Vocabulary

remonstrance (103)	pall (104)	fortnight (106)	timorous (107)
scullery (108)	rampart (110)	impetus (111)	vogue (112)
integument (112)	cerebral (112)	tactile (113)	carnivorous (113)
physiological (113)	salient (115)		

Discussion Questions

1. Discuss the activities and the relationship of the narrator and the curate. *(The Black Smoke hems them in for two days in a deserted house. When the smoke lifts, the narrator's concern for his wife prompts him to proceed. The curate wants to remain but consents to go when he sees the narrator's determination. They observe Martian destruction everywhere and finally find food and take refuge in another deserted house. The fifth cylinder lands on the house, and the Martians surround it. The two men are undetected but are imprisoned in the scullery. The narrator grows weary of the curate's selfishness and whining and wishes he had gone alone. pp. 103-109)*

2. Describe the Martian fighting machines and their occupants. *(Machine: like a metallic spider with five jointed legs and many tentacles; coordinated and animated as if alive. Occupants: huge round bodies, primarily heads with a face in front; face has no nostrils but a pair of large dark eyes, sixteen tentacles around mouth (their "hands"); fleshy beak; surface resembling an ear in back of head; greater part of structure is a brain with nerves to eyes, ear, and tentacles; has heart and veins; mouth opens into lungs; wear no clothing. pp. 111-113, 116)*

3. Discuss how the Martians feed. Analyze the statement, "The bare idea of this is no doubt horribly repulsive to us, but at the same time I think that we should remember how repulsive our carnivorous habits would seem to an intelligent rabbit." Note prior reference to eating on p. 77. *(They eat by injecting fresh blood of living creatures into their own veins. Discuss with students what Wells' reference to carnivorous eating habits might suggest about his view of humankind. Responses will vary. p. 113)*

4. Examine the physiological differences between men and Martians and the possible effects these differences may have on the Martians who have landed on the earth. *(Martians do not sleep, are absolutely without sex, and have never been exposed to disease. Possible effects: can keep constant vigil because of needing no sleep; note reproduction of Martian on p. 114—"budded off"; having no disease foreshadows their eventual demise. pp. 114-115)*

5. Note the reference to the rapid growth of the red weed (p. 115). Continue to note references to the red weed for future discussion.

Supplementary Activities

1. Note the allusion to Pompeii on p. 104. Bring to class pictures of the destruction of Pompeii and compare with the destruction of the Martians.

2. Have student volunteers sketch a Martian fighting machine and its occupant or develop this as a composite class drawing (e.g., a mural).

3. Have students discuss or write an essay about the narrator. What traits does he possess that have kept him alive thus far? How might he represent the strongest of the species?

4. Note the similes: country was as though a black snowstorm had passed over it (p. 104); it [the earth] behaved like mud under violent blow of a hammer (p. 111); vapor drove up like a veil across peephole (p. 111).

Chapters 3-6, pp. 118-133

The narrator and the curate continue to hide in the collapsed house and to observe the Martians. Other fighting machines arrive. The Martians detect, capture, and kill the curate.

Vocabulary

accentuated (118)	efficacious (118)	importunities (118)	oscillatory (119)
enigma (121)	vestiges (121)	rudimentary (123)	paradoxical (124)
copiously (126)	infinity (126)		

Discussion Questions

1. Discuss the feelings the narrator has toward the curate. Analyze the universality of how close proximity with another person reveals personality flaws and often leads to open conflict. *(He believes them to be absolutely incompatible, he hates his endless muttering, and he resents the impulsive way the curate eats and drinks as well as his carelessness. He thinks the curate is silly and weak. pp. 118-119)*

2. Examine how the observance of the Martians' feeding habits affects the two men and leads inadvertently to the curate's death. *(The curate is so traumatized that he loses all reasoning ability and begins to drink more of the stored liquor, leading to eventual open conflict between the two men. The narrator becomes more determined to escape, and observing the curate's insanity strengthens and keeps him sane. The curate becomes loud and uncontrollable, and the narrator knocks him out but not before a Martian hears the curate, searches for him with its tentacle, and seizes him. The narrator barely escapes. pp. 120-126)*

3. Discuss the narrator's escape from the house, what he observes, and its effect on him. Have students speculate on what it would be like if "the fear and empire of man passes away." *(On the fifteenth day of his isolation, he looks through the peephole and realizes all the Martians are gone, and he escapes. He observes a multitude of red cactus-shaped plants covering everything but no other plant growth, dead trees, wrecked houses, and human skeletons. As he proceeds, the red plants form a swamp, and he finds patches of wreckage interspersed with undisturbed areas. The red weed gradually becomes less abundant. He finds neither humans nor Martians. He feels that he is on another planet and that the empire of man has passed away. pp. 128-133)*

4. **Predictions:** Where are the Martians? What will happen to the narrator?

Supplementary Activities
1. Have students analyze the curate's allusions to the wine press of God and to "Woe...to the inhabitants of the earth..." on p. 124, noting his self-blame for the Martians' invasion. Reference: Bible, Isaiah 63:36; Revelation 14:19-20 and 8:13. Both allusions relate to end-time Apocalyptic prophecies.

2. Note the similes: he was as lacking in restraint as a silly woman (p. 118); faint metallic ringing like movements of keys on a split-ring (p. 125), the Thing—like an elephant's trunk...like a black worm (p. 126)

Chapters 7-8, pp. 134-155
The narrator joins forces with the soldier he had previously met in Maybury but leaves him when he realizes the insanity of the soldier's plans for survival. The narrator enters London and discovers dead Martians, indicating that the terror is over.

Vocabulary
fetish (135)	languid (136)	eroticism (141)	parleyed (142)
cloaca (144)	reconnoitre (144)	euchre (146)	kinetic (146)
spectrally (151)	temerity (151)	redoubt (152)	

Discussion Questions
1. Discuss the three things that struggle for possession of the narrator's mind and possible resolution of each. *(Killing of the curate, whereabouts of the Martians, possible fate of his wife. Resolution: Responses will vary. Suggestions include: death of curate—absolve himself of all blame; whereabouts of Martians—retrace his steps rather than go forward since he has found no trace of Martians for several miles; his wife—return to Leatherhead and try to find her. pp. 134-135)*

2. Discuss what the narrator learns from the soldier with whom he joins forces. Analyze the mental state of the soldier and what causes the narrator eventually to leave him. Discuss meaning of the term "pipe dream" and have students relate incidents of pipe dreams. *(He learns the Martians have gone to London, are apparently building a flying machine, only one Martian has been killed, and they seem to be preparing for others to arrive. The soldier believes the humans are defeated and that the Martians will make pets of them, eating them when they are ready. The soldier plans to live in the sewers under London, building a society that will save*

humanity, staying out of the Martians' way and leaving them alone. The narrator at first believes in the plausibility of the plan but begins to detect flaws in the soldier such as his laziness, drunkenness, and plan to capture a Martian fighting machine. The narrator resolves to leave the soldier because of the insanity of the soldier's actions and plan. pp. 134-147)

3. Examine implications of what the narrator finds as he proceeds toward London. *(Although the red weed is still everywhere, its fronds show signs of spreading disease that will eventually destroy it. Black dust covers everything, including several dead bodies. As he gets closer to London, the narrator hears a strange wailing and observes a stationary, howling Martian. He finds a wrecked machine and dead Martians. He realizes they have died because of the human disease bacteria that has invaded their systems and against which they have no defense. The Martian invasion has ended. pp. 148-155)*

4. **Predictions:** Will the narrator find his wife? What will he find when he returns home?

Supplementary Activities

1. Have a student research and report to the class the story of Samson in the Bible, Judges 13:1-16:31. Analyze the allusion to Samson and compare his reign and demise with that of the Martians.

2. Refer to the phrase, "the huge fighting machine that would fight no more forever" (p. 153) and compare to a statement in the 1877 speech of surrender to the United States Army of Indian Nez Perce Chief Joseph. He stated, "My heart is sick and sad. From where the sun now stands, I will fight no more forever." Have students compare/contrast the defeat of the Indians with the demise of the Martians.

3. Note the literary devices: **Metaphors**—we're [humans] eatable ants (p. 138); germs: microscopic allies (p. 153). **Similes**—I crept out of the house like a rat leaving its hiding place (p. 135); I went for the Martians like a sparrow goes for man (p. 139); black as a sweep (p. 148); windows...like eye sockets in skulls (p. 151); people... like sheep without a shepherd (p. 154) **Personification**—London was lying in state in its black shroud (p. 150); Night...mother of fear and mystery (p. 151); Angel of Death (p. 153); London...mother of cities (p. 154) **Allusion**—Sennacherib (p. 153) Bible, 2 Kings 19:35-37, referred to in a poem, "Sennacherib" by Lord Byron

Chapters 9-10, pp. 156-164

England rejoices and the world responds to the need. The narrator returns to his home in Maybury and finds his wife alive.

Vocabulary

inane (157)   morbidity (157)   vestries (158)   putrefactive (161)

Discussion Questions

1. Discuss the reaction to the fall of the Martians. Compare the response to England's need with today's world-wide response to disasters such as famine and floods. *(Bells ring all over England, comparable to end of World War II. People rejoice and offer help to the haggard refugees. Other countries ship an abundance of food to London. pp. 155-158)*

2. Examine what the narrator learns about Leatherhead and what he finds when he returns to his home after his four week absence. Ask students to relate any incidents in which they returned to their homes after a disaster such as a storm or fire. *(Leatherhead and all its inhabitants have been destroyed. He finds heaped masses of red weed, the Union Jack flying over the mass of earth about a cylinder, his house desolate, and his wife, alive. pp. 158-160)*

3. Analyze the irony of the paper the narrator finds on his desk when he returns home. Note the subject matter and the significance of the last sentence. *(Subject: Probable development of moral ideas with the development of the civilizing process. Last sentence: In about two hundred years, we may expect... He was working on the paper, left to get the newspaper, and heard about the "Men from Mars." Responses will vary. Ask students to analyze whether or not Wells wrote* The War of the Worlds *as a prophecy and/or a warning. pp. 159-160)*

4. Discuss what happens in the epilogue and how the narrator now views his world. *(Examination of the dead Martians leads to the conclusion that they died because of bacteria and that they did not understand the decaying process since they buried none of their own. Analysis of the Black Smoke is inconclusive but points to a mixture of deadly gasses. No longer does the earth seem secure from invasion by other species. The narrator is left with a sense of doubt and insecurity, and he suffers from nightmares about the devastation. He treasures life and, above all, the ability to once again hold his wife's hand. pp. 161-164)*

Supplementary Activities

1. Note the simile on p. 157, "He had swept it [Leatherhead] out of existence...as a boy might crush an ant hill in the mere wantonness of power."

2. Have students bring to class pictures or articles concerning the after-effects of the bombing of Nagasaki and Hiroshima. Discuss the ravages of atomic warfare and compare with the destruction in the novel.

3. Have students write a short poem beginning with the line, "Ghosts of the past linger..."

4. Have students create a list of things they would treasure following such an ordeal. Discuss as a class.

Post-reading Discussion Questions

1. Using the character chart on page 20 of this guide, discuss the characters in the novel.

2. Place "Martians Invade England" in the center oval of an attribute web (page 21 of this guide). Place the names of characters on the long lines and discuss and record the characters' reactions to the invasion.

3. The characterization graphic on page 22 of this guide can be used to analyze any character in the book. Have a student fill in the rectangles and ovals as the class brainstorms about individual characters.

4. Place a story map (page 23 of this guide) on an overhead transparency. Divide students into small groups and have them record their observations. Have a spokesperson for each group identify the various components of the novel.

5. Discuss and summarize the novel using the novel web diagram on page 24 of this guide.

6. Analyze the chapters devoted to the experiences of the narrator's brother (Book One, Chapters 14, 16, and 17). Ask students whether or not they think Wells' technique is effective. Speculate on what might have happened to the narrator's brother and the two women after they escaped the Martian.

7. Compare the death of the Martians with actual human deaths from diseases such as the bubonic plague or AIDS. Discuss the importance of a human's immune system and what might happen if that is destroyed.

8. Compare and contrast the Martians in this novel with aliens in other works the students have read or in movies they have seen.

9. Analyze the importance of the Martians' large brains.

10. Note Wells' reference to the Martians' lack of sex. Discuss a common view in the 1900s that sexual desire was the lowest of human emotions.

11. Discuss whether or not students think *The War of the Worlds* was prophetic in nature and if Wells actually believed Martians would some day invade the world.

12. Discuss whether or not students think H. G. Wells was the "father of modern science fiction." Analyze the development of the genre, including the *Star Trek* and *Star Wars* productions.

13. Examine different beliefs about the destruction of the earth. Discuss scientific, religious, personal, and other veiwpoints.

© Novel Units, Inc.   All rights reserved

Post-reading Extension Activities

Note: The instructions for the extension activities are directed toward the student and can be used as a handout. Each student should complete at least one extension assignment.

Writing
1. Research and write a three-page report about Mars. Identify facts from the exposition of the novel.
2. Write a poem of at least 18 lines titled, "They're Coming!"
3. Write a series of journal entries beginning with "I am the last man (or woman) alive."
4. Write a new ending for the novel.
5. Write a lament from the viewpoint of the last living Martian.
6. Write a news article about the final destruction of the Martians.

Viewing
1. View the 1953 movie version of *The War of the Worlds*. Give an oral report to the class comparing and contrasting the novel and the film.
2. View another science fiction movie. Write or give an oral report in which you compare and contrast the aliens in the movie with the Martians in *The War of the Worlds.*

Listening/Speaking
1. Listen to a tape of the 1938 Orson Welles' radio production of *The War of the Worlds*. This can be either from the original or a reproduction. Research and report to the class on the context of the script and the effect this broadcast had on the nation.
2. Write and present to the class your own monologue of your impression of the Martian's motives.

Art
1. Create a collage that depicts the invasion of the Martians.
2. Prepare a series of sketches showing highlights of the book.
3. Prepare a pen and ink drawing of a Martian.

Drama
Write and present to the class a skit taken from one of the dramatic sections of the novel.

Music
1. Select and play background music that enhances your oral reading of an emotional portion of the novel.
2. Write and perform a ballad about the demise of the Martians.

Character Chart

Directions: Fill in character names supplied by your teacher across the top boxes. In the boxes across from each of the feelings, describe an incident or time in the book when each character felt that way. You may use "not applicable" if you cannot find an example.

Feeling				
Frustration				
Anger				
Fear				
Humiliation				
Relief				
Admiration				

Attribute Web

Directions: In the center oval, record a significant event, place, or object from the book. Each major character goes on the five long lines. The smaller lines are for that particular character's reaction to the significant event, place, or object.

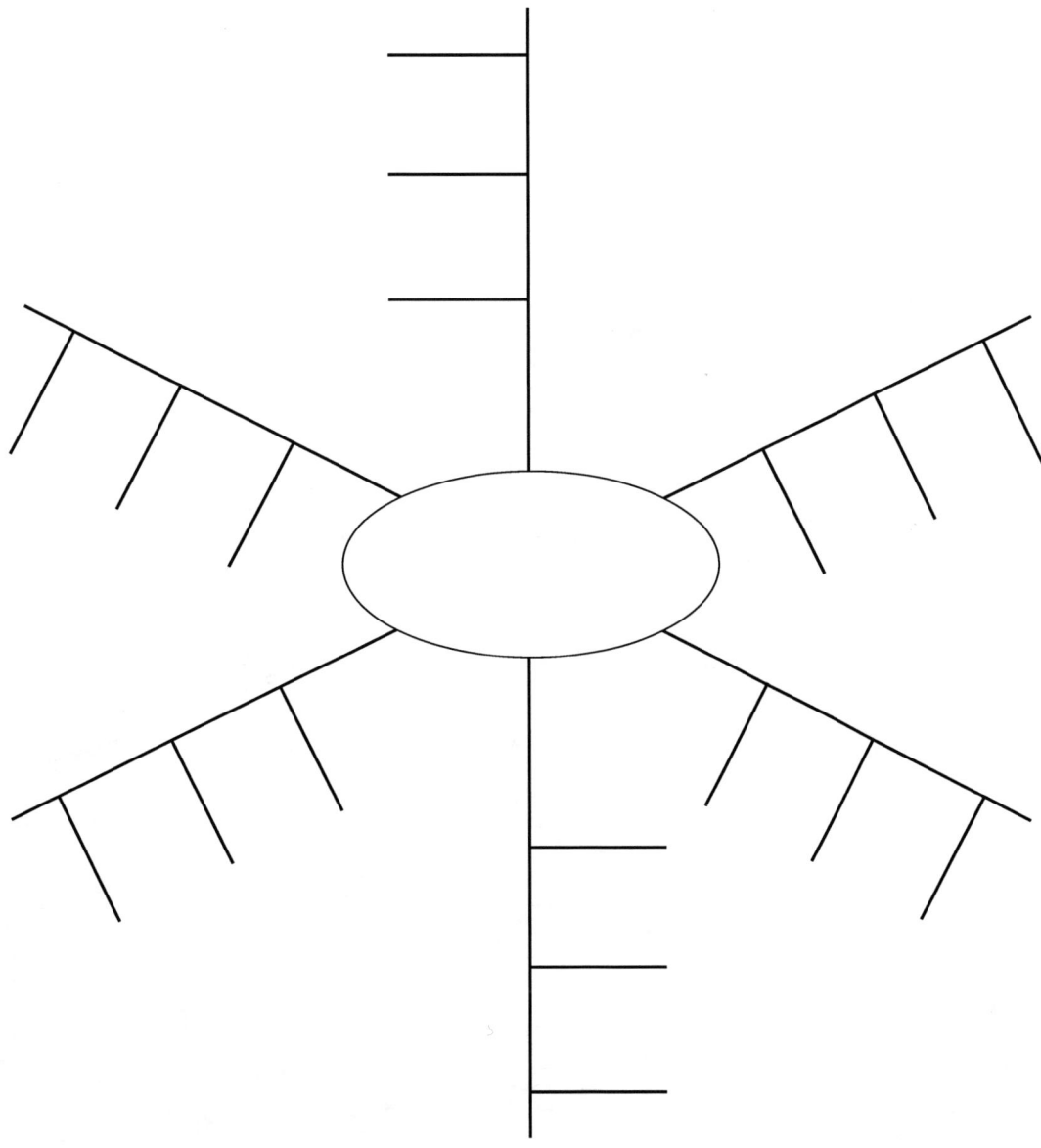

Characterization

Directions: Write a character's name in the center. Place in each oval an adjective that describes him/her. Fill in each rectangle with a supporting detail from the novel.

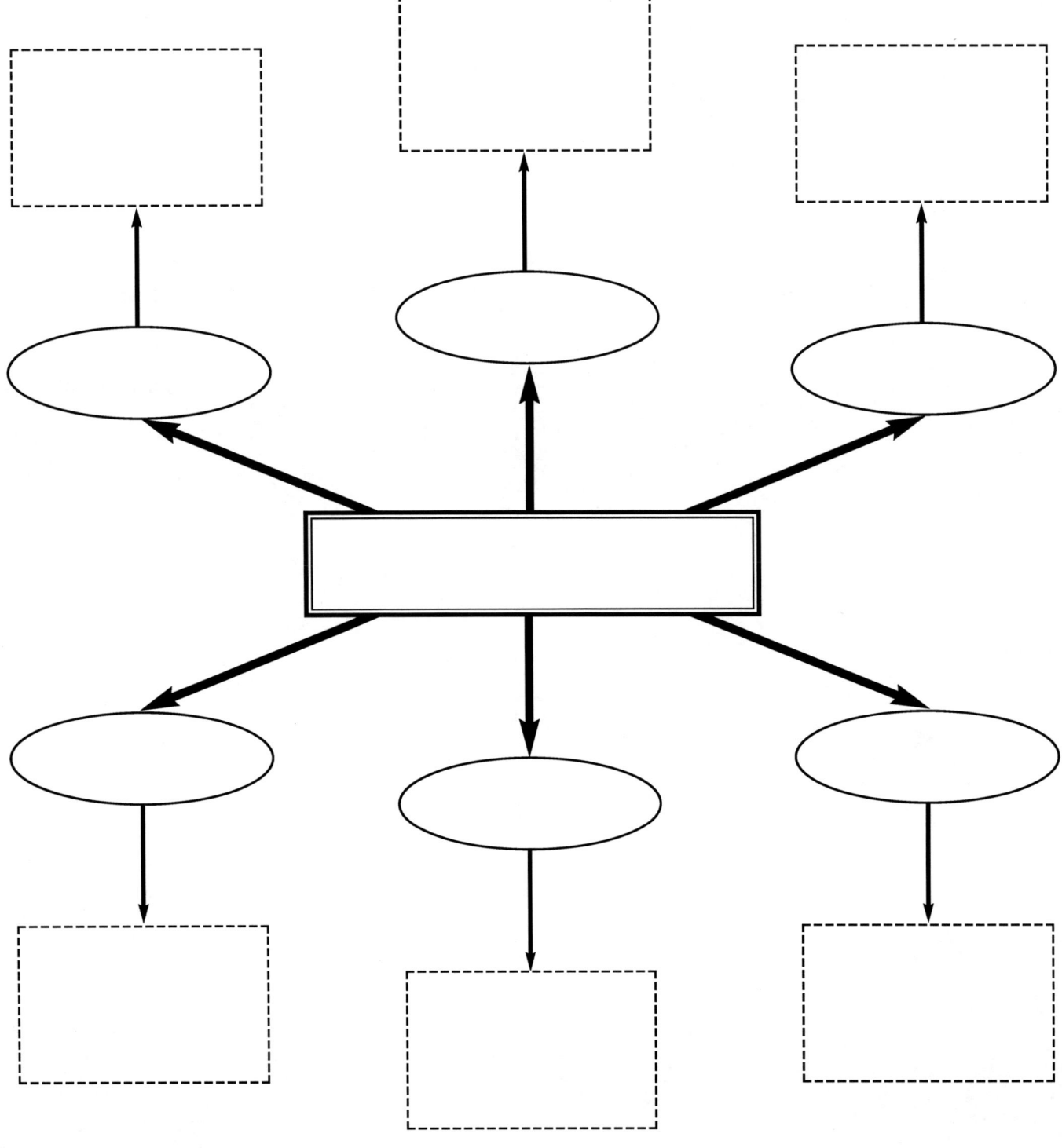

Story Map

Settings/Main Characters

Statement of the Problem

Event 1

Event 2

Event 3

Event 4

Event 5

Statement of the Solution

Story Theme (What is the author really trying to tell us about people in general?)

Novel Web Diagram

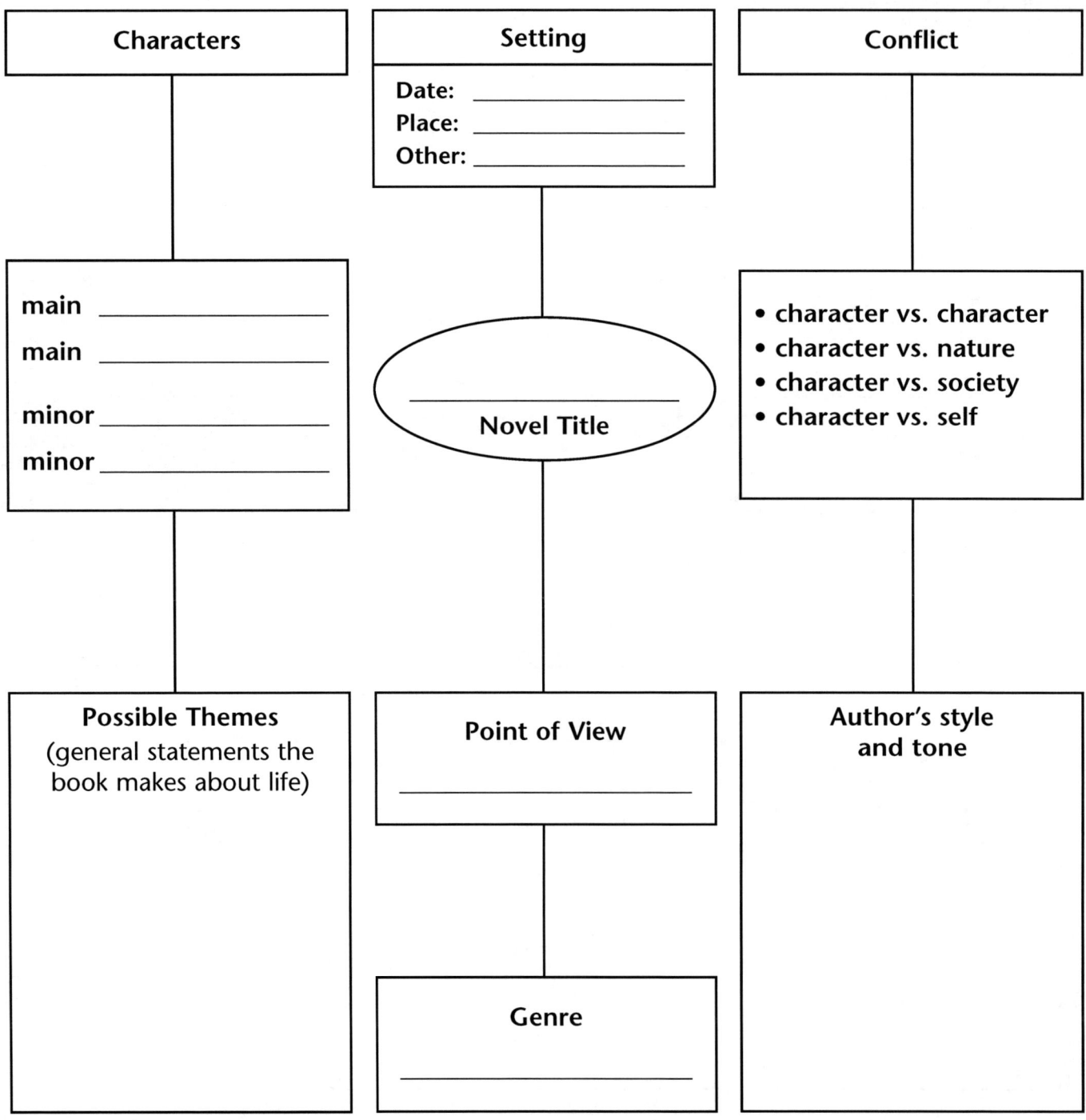

Assessment for *The War of the Worlds*

Assessment is an ongoing process. The following ten items can be completed during the novel study. Once finished, the student and teacher will check the work. Points may be added to indicate the level of understanding.

Name _____ Date _____

Student   **Teacher**

_____   _____   1. Correct any exams or quizzes taken over the novel.

_____   _____   2. Write two review questions over the novel and use these to participate in an oral review.

_____   _____   3. Write a review of the novel.

_____   _____   4. Display or perform your extension projects on an assigned day.

_____   _____   5. Using examples from the book, respond orally to the themes "survival" and "fear."

_____   _____   6. Write a one-word response as the teacher calls out the names of various characters.

_____   _____   7. Write an example of each: metaphor, simile, allusion, and personification.

_____   _____   8. Discuss the types of conflict found in the novel. Provide examples from the novel.

_____   _____   9. Explain Wells' work as "prophetic" citing examples from the novel (e.g., gas warfare, laser weapons).

_____   _____   10. Compare your completed story maps and character charts in small groups of three or four.

© Novel Units, Inc.   All rights reserved

Glossary

Book One

Chapters 1-3, pp. 3-15
1. mortal (3): sure to die; of or characterized by death
2. nebular (3): of or having to do with a nebular (mass of dust particles or gases or cloud-like cluster of stars)
3. attenuated (4): weakened in force, amount, or value; reduced
4. heath (9): area of uncultivated land with heather or low bushes growing on it
5. incrustation (10): crust or hard coating
6. cylinder (11): a solid bounded by two equal, parallel circles, and a curved surface
7. astronomical (13): having to do with astronomy (the science of the sun, moon, planets, stars, and all other celestial bodies)
8. oxide (14): compound of oxygen with another element or radical
9. extraterrestrial (14): outside or originating away from the earth and its atmosphere

Chapters 4-6, pp. 16-25
1. terrestrial (17): of the earth
2. aperture (18): opening, gap, hole
3. apex (19): highest point; top
4. intimation (20): indirect suggestion; hint
5. deputation (20): group of persons sent to represent others; delegation
6. parabolic (23): having the form of a parabola (plane curve formed by intersection of a cone with a plane parallel to the side of the cone)

Chapters 7-9, pp. 26-38
1. incongruity (27): condition of being out of place; unfitness; inappropriateness
2. erethism (29): excessive or abnormal amount of irritability or stimulation in an organ or tissue
3. canard (30): unfounded rumor; exaggerated report; hoax
4. indefatigable (32): never getting tired or giving up
5. cordon (32): line or circle of soldiers, policemen, or others acting to enclose or guard a place
6. lassitude (33): lack of energy; feeling of weakness; weariness

Chapters 10-11, pp. 39-49
1. insensate (42): without sensation; lifeless; inanimate
2. repugnance (43): strong dislike, distaste, or aversion
3. conflagration (45): large, destructive fire
4. lethargy (46): drowsiness, dullness; lack of energy

Chapters 12-13, pp. 50-64
1. theodolite (51): surveying instrument for measuring horizontal and vertical angles
2. heliograph (51): device for signaling by means of a movable mirror that flashes beams of sunlight to a distance

3. assiduously (52): working hard and steadily; carefully; attentively; diligently
4. omnibus (53): large vehicle with seats inside and sometimes also on the roof
5. sabbatical (53): of or suitable for the Sabbath
6. obliquely (55): indirectly, slantingly
7. curate (62): assistant clergyman

Chapters 14-15, pp. 65-81
1. menagerie (67): collection of wild animals
2. terminus (68): either end of a railroad line
3. quasi (70): not real; seemingly but not actually the same as; halfway
4. nomadic (71): wandering, roving
5. tocsin (72): alarm sounded by ringing a bell or bells; warning signal
6. ejaculating (74): exclaiming or saying suddenly
7. ululation (76): howl or wail

Chapters 16-17, pp. 82-100
1. coherency (82): logically connected
2. stalwart (83): strongly or stoutly built; sturdy, robust
3. pugilistic (84): having to do with boxing or boxers
4. paroxysm (86): sudden outburst of emotion or activity
5. torpor (89): apathy, lethargy, listlessness, dullness
6. volition (92): act of willing; decision or choice
7. rout (93): disorderly retreat of defeated troops
8. ramifications (94): a dividing or spreading out in branches or parts
9. chaffering (96): disputing about a price; bargaining
10. exorbitant (97): extravagant; excessive degree or amount; beyond reasonable doubt
11. leviathan (98): sea monster, very large or powerful object

Book Two
Chapters 1-2, pp. 103-117
1. remonstrance (103): protest, complaint
2. pall (104): dark, gloomy covering
3. fortnight (106): two weeks
4. timorous (107): easily frightened; timid
5. scullery (108): small room where dirty, rough work of kitchen is done
6. rampart (110): wide bank of earth, often with a wall or top, built for defense
7. impetus (111): driving force or impulse
8. vogue (112): popular use; prevailing fashion

© Novel Units, Inc.   All rights reserved

9. integument (112): natural outer covering
10. cerebral (112): of the brain
11. tactile (113): having to do with the sense of touch
12. carnivorous (113): feeding chiefly on flesh; using other animals as food
13. physiological (113): having to do with the functions of living organisms and their parts
14. salient (115): standing out; easily seen or noticed; prominent

Chapters 3-6, pp. 118-133
1. accentuated (118): called special attention to; emphasized, intensified
2. efficacious (118): producing desired results; effective
3. importunities (118): urgent or repeated requests
4. oscillatory (119): swaying to and fro like a pendulum
5. enigma (121): baffling or puzzling problem, situation, or person; riddle or paradox
6. vestiges (121): all that remains; slight remnants or traces
7. rudimentary (123): that which is to be learned or studied first; elementary
8. paradoxical (124): having to do with statements that may be true but seem to say two opposite things; having contradictory qualities
9. copiously (126): plentifully, abundantly
10. infinity (126): condition of being infinite (without limits or bounds; endless)

Chapters 7-8, pp. 134-155
1. fetish (135): anything regarded with unreasoning reverence or blind devotion
2. languid (136): feeling weak; without energy
3. eroticism (141): erotic (sexual passion or love) character or tendency
4. parleyed (142): discussed with an enemy
5. cloaca (144): sewer
6. reconnoitre (144): to inspect or survey an area to gather information
7. euchre (146): simple card game
8. kinetic (146): of or having to do with motion
9. spectrally (151): ghostly
10. temerity (151): reckless boldness; rashness
11. redoubt (152): small, usually temporary fort

Chapters 9-10, pp. 156-164
1. inane (157): silly or foolish; senseless
2. morbidity (157): unhealthy, sickly condition or quality
3. vestries (158): committees of church members
4. putrefactive (161): causing to rot or decay